The Tiger Who Came To Tea

Text and Illustrations

by

Kathy Creamer

SINGAPORE
OXFORD UNIVERSITY PRESS
1996

"Raffles Hotel is one of the most famous hotels in the world. Many important people have stayed here. Sultans and kings, prime ministers and politicians, writers and artists, film stars and musicians all like to say that they've visited Raffles Hotel.

I'd like to tell you an old story about one particular visitor to Raffles, an unusual visitor who was not at all welcome. He came to rather a sad end ... but he succeeded in making himself very famous indeed!"

One very hot day, long, long ago, in old Singapore, there was a hungry, hungry tiger who decided to pay a visit to the famous Raffles Hotel. *"I wonder what's on the menu?"* said the tiger as he sniffed the warm air. *"I'd like something really tasty for my tea."*

The tiger walked softly and silently up the white marble steps of the big hotel. The jagah and the bellboy couldn't believe their eyes when they saw the tiger creeping into the hallway. They both hid behind a big, potted palm until the hungry, hungry tiger passed them by.

Then they ran as fast as their legs could carry them, to tell the hotel manager and Major Blunder, the great hunter, about the tiger.

5

The hungry, hungry tiger prowled about in the corridor until he found the Tiffin Room. The room was full of hotel guests who were sitting at beautifully laid tables and tucking into all sorts of delicious food from the Raffles Hotel kitchen.

There was spicy Tiffin curry with crispy *poppadums* and tasty chutney, succulent roast beef and Yorkshire pudding with lashings of gravy, sweet chicken *satay* and fragrant rice, shrimp noodles, peppered rump steak with French fries and hot *nasi goreng* with a lot of chilli!

"*Mmmmh!*" said the tiger as he licked his lips. He opened his huge jaws and roared his loudest roar!

All the people in the Tiffin Room stopped eating and stared in horror at the hungry, hungry tiger. Then there was a lot of loud crashing and smashing of plates and cups and glasses and bowls as the people began to run out of the room!

"Help! There's a hungry, hungry tiger!" they all screamed. *"It's going to eat us!"*

Some people hid under their chairs while others jumped up on the tables and climbed onto the big chandeliers.

But the hungry, hungry tiger wasn't interested in eating people. He could smell something far more delicious, something that Raffles Hotel was very famous for…Tiffin curry!

He sat down at a table and helped himself to a big plate of spicy curry, which he gobbled up, all in one great mouthful. He ate up all the *poppadums* and all the chutney too.

Next he ate all the succulent roast beef and all the Yorkshire pudding, and drank all the gravy.

He swallowed up all the hot *nasi goreng*.
He chomped all the peppered steak with French fries.
He gorged on all the shrimp noodles.
He crunched his way through all the sweet chicken *satay*, and he even ate the *satay* sticks! He didn't waste a single scrap!

The tiger kept on eating until he wasn't hungry any more! He sat back in his chair and burped an enormous burp.

"I'm stuffed," he growled, "but now I'm thirsty! That nasi goreng was full of chilli. I need a cool drink."

The thirsty, thirsty tiger sniffed the air.

"*There's water nearby,*" he growled and off he went, following his nose. Just as the tiger disappeared round a corner, the hotel manager, Major Blunder, the jagah and the bellboy burst into the Tiffin Room.

The hotel manager was in his pyjamas because he had attended the Raffles Hotel fancy dress ball the night before, and had only just gone to bed! *"Has anybody here seen a tiger?"* asked the hotel manager, rubbing his sleepy red eyes.

"*Yes!*" said all the trembling guests, "*It went that way!*"
And they all pointed in the direction in which the tiger had gone.

15

"Don't worry. By Jove, I'm a famous hunter!" boasted Major Blunder. "I've shot hundreds of tigers in India, I'll have you know. I'm a crack shot, what!"

"Did he say he was a crack shot or a crackpot?" asked a man who was dangling from a chandelier.

"I'll soon blast the blighter!" said Major Blunder, waving a huge shotgun in the air. "Tally hoe, what!"

The hotel manager, Major Blunder, the jagah and the bellboy began to track the tiger along the cool corridors of the hotel.

Meanwhile, the thirsty, thirsty tiger prowled around the palm-fringed verandahs outside. He crept up to a man who was lying

in the sun on one of the long-chairs. The man had also been to the fancy dress ball the night before. He had enjoyed himself so much that he didn't want to go to bed! He had fallen asleep on the long-chair instead, and was now snoring loudly!

"*What a noise!*" said the tiger to himself. "*He sounds just like a warthog!*" The tiger sniffed the man just to make quite sure that he wasn't really a warthog and then went on his way.

Soon he came to the Palm Court garden, where the hotel guests were sitting in the sun drinking Singapore Slings and listening to a man playing the piano. The tiger licked his lips. He opened his huge jaws and roared an enormous roar!

"Help! A tiger!" screamed all the people. *"A savage tiger!"*
Glasses smashed and tables crashed as people jumped up and ran away. Some of them climbed up the palm trees, and the man playing the piano jumped into it and shut the lid with a bang!

19

But the tiger wasn't interested in them. He just wanted a long cool drink! He spotted the hotel swimming pool and bounded over to the sparkling blue water. Then he crouched and lapped the water nosily.

At that moment, the hotel manager, Major Blunder, the jagah and the bellboy arrived at the scene.

"By thunder, we've got the blighter!" yelled Major Blunder as
he raised his shotgun and peered down the barrel.
The tiger looked up, just in time to see Major Blunder point his
shotgun at him and take aim!

The tiger turned and raced away like lightning across the Palm Court garden and into the bushes. Then he was gone.

"Oh, bad luck old man!" said Major Blunder. "He's using camouflage tactics now. We'll just have to flush him out, what!"

The hotel manager, Major Blunder, the jagah and the bellboy bravely followed the tiger.

They tracked the tiger by following its huge footprints through the bushes and under the billiard room floor. The billiard room was on stilts like many of the buildings in old Singapore. But there, the footprints faded.

"*Blast it! We've lost the trail, old boy,*" said Major Blunder, looking very disappointed.

"*Never mind,*" said the hotel manager. "*Let's hope he's gone back into the jungle where he belongs.*"

The hotel manager, Major Blunder, the jagah and the bellboy all began to walk back towards the Palm Court garden. Little did they know that the tiger was now tracking ... them!

Suddenly, there came a ferocious growl from behind the bougainvillea bushes, and a pair of bright green eyes peered out at them all.

"There's the blighter!" yelled Major Blunder. *"I'll get him this time!"*

Major Blunder quickly took aim with his shotgun and fired.

Bang! Bang! But he missed.

The tiger was now furious at being shot at and he leaped out at them, growling, snarling and ready to sink his sharp teeth into the first person he could catch!

But this time the hotel manager raised his gun and pulled the trigger.

Blam! Blam! And that was the sad end of the hungry, thirsty tiger!

All the hotel guests came to look at the big dead tiger, lying stretched out on the lalang.

"What a beautiful animal!" said the hotel manager. "It's a great shame that I had to shoot him, but he might've killed one of us."

"Just look at his golden coat and thick black tiger stripes!" said the bellboy.
"What huge sharp white teeth and long whiskers!" said the jagah.
"And oh, just look at those enormous feet, as big as dinner plates!" said the hotel guests.

"Yes, he was an attractive chap," said Major Blunder. "Rotten shame we had to pop him off, what! But he might have eaten someone for tea. Never mind, there are many more tigers in the jungle."

"Now this story happened a long, long time ago, when there were indeed many thousands of tigers living in the jungle, and nobody would have missed one hungry, thirsty tiger at all! But today, in our modern world, the tiger is an animal in danger of becoming extinct.

There are now very few tigers left in our world and each day, more disappear. They are losing their jungle habitat and are still being hunted for their beautiful coats, shiny sharp teeth and huge bones. By the end of this century, the beautiful tiger could become extinct, just like the dinosaurs!

Organisations like the World Wildlife Fund are fighting to save the tiger and many other animals from extinction.

Now, if the hungry, thirsty tiger came to tea at Raffles Hotel today, it would be a very different story indeed! The zoo would be called in to capture the tiger safely. The tiger would then be taken to his own jungle compound within the zoo. There he would be looked after by his keepers and would be fed and well cared for. And while the zoo-keepers were on their way to collect the tiger from Raffles Hotel, the hotel staff would feed him a sumptuous Raffles tea.

When the tiger finished gobbling up all the wonderful gourmet food, he would certainly want to quote the famous author, Rudyard Kipling, who always said, ' "When in Singapore … " '.

This book is for
Anna & David Tandy.

Oxford University Press
Oxford New York
Athens Auckland Bangkok Bombay
Calcutta Cape Town Dar es Salaam Delhi
Florence Hong Kong Istanbul Karachi Kuala Lumpur
Madras Madrid Melbourne Mexico City
Nairobi Paris Singapore Taipei Tokyo Toronto

and associated companies in
Berlin Ibadan

Oxford is a trademark of Oxford University Press
© Oxford University Press 1996

This edition is specially published for Raffles Hotel
1 Beach Road, Singapore 189673

ISBN 0 19 588106 0

Printed by KHL Printing Pte Ltd
Designed by FSTOP Pte Ltd
Published by Oxford University Press Pte Ltd
37 Jalan Pemimpin, #03-03 Union Industrial Building, Block A, Singapore 577177